Franklin File, Edward P. Call

Supremacy

A Drama in Four Acts

Franklin File, Edward P. Call

Supremacy
A Drama in Four Acts

ISBN/EAN: 9783337343323

Printed in Europe, USA, Canada, Australia, Japan

Cover: Foto ©Andreas Hilbeck / pixelio.de

More available books at **www.hansebooks.com**

IN FOUR ACTS.

BY

FRANKLIN FILE AND EDWARD P. CALL.

———

———

BOSTON:

MILLS, KNIGHT & CO., PRINTERS, 115 CONGRESS STREET.

1881.

CHARACTERS.

HERR BRENNER.

RUDOLPH BRENNER. [*His son.*]

BARON ROTHBART.

HAROLD. [*His son.*]

CRISTA BRENNER. [*Baroness Rothbart, his daughter.*]

MAX REIMER. [*Master miner at the Brenner coal mines.*]

MEYER KELLNER.

MINA.

CARL.

PAUL.   } [*Miners.*]

CRAFTMAN.

OLD REIMER. [*Max's father.*]

ANTON and FRANZ. [*Servants at Brenner mansion.*]

HERR KLASSEN. [*Director at mines.*]

HERR WEBER. [*Engineer at mines.*]

SCENE. — *The interior of Germany.*

TIME. — *The present.*

SUPREMACY.

ACT I.

Scene. — *The exterior of the Brenner mansion at the Brenner mines. The sun has just set, and during the first half of the act it darkens to night, and the moon rises thereafter. The portion of the house which is seen shows that it is old fashioned and elegant. House is set across the corner, L. U. — hills in distance. The stage is lighted a soft green, and at no time during the act are the lights more than one-fourth up.*

Curtain rises, disclosing Kellner, *the* Director, *and from a dozen to twenty miners, dressed in an appropriate way for the reception of the bridal couple. Also five or six women, among them being* Mina. *The men and women have branches and wreaths in their hands, but their expressions do not denote much interest in the festivities.* Kellner *and* Director *at back.*

Craftman. I tell you it is so; and before this newly-married couple, now on their way from the city, have seen the end of their sweet honeymoon, all that I have said, if not more, will prove true.

Paul. Well, be it so or not, you should not think aloud on this occasion.

Craft. [*Sneeringly.*] *This occasion* — bah! Just because we must come and seem kind toward Herr Brenner and his useless son, does it follow that I must choke and smother my own feelings? You're chicken-hearted, Paul, from head to foot.

Paul. Wait until the revolt you predict breaks out, and then see how chicken-hearted I am.   [*Goes up.*

Director. How now, Craftman, what's in the wind
with you?

Craft. Nothing, Herr Director, nothing, nothing.

Director. [*Quietly eyeing him.*] Ah, "nothing"!
which, being translated, means "a great deal."

[*Craftman goes up.*

Kellner. [*Coming forward with Mina.*] By my
troth, Director [*looking at watch*], the party is overdue
some forty minutes, and Mina here says the train
arrived at Valley Station promptly.

Mina. Yes, Herr Director, for the arrival of the
train was to have been the signal for Max to march
with his men, and I have seen them start.

Director. Can you not see the carriage-way from
the porch? Look, Herr Kellner!

Kellner. Come up, Mina!

[*They go to porch of house. They look off.*

Director. Well, do you see the carriages?

Mina. Yes, there are two together; it is time to
make ready.   [*Starts to come down.*

Kellner. Stop, wait, look! The third carriage is
ahead, and not behind.   [*Spirited.*

Mina. Yes, yes, and see how rapidly it drives?

Director. [*Now looking.*] Great Heavens, the horses
are past control; they are tearing madly!

Kellner. [*Breathlessly.*] A rod from their course
will pitch the carriage into the valley!

Director. 'Tis Herr Rudolph's!

Mina. Look, look, there's Max! What—no—he
dare not! Yes, he dashes toward the road.

Kellner. And now see, he's going to seize the horses!

Director. He springs like a tiger!

Mina. Yes, he has their bridles!

Kellner. My soul, just see them drag him!

Mina. But he keeps his hold!

Director. Alas! some one is thrown from the carriage.

Kellner. Yes — Herr Rudolph —

Mina. Oh! but now they yield as they approach
the gateway. Yes, they are still. Max raises himself
and assists her ladyship. The others join them. May
we go, Herr Klassen, and try to help them?

Director. By all means — those who will. [*Exeunt all but Paul and Craftman, the former being beckoned by the latter.*

Paul. What is it, Craftman? What have you to say to Max's being the savior of the "useless son" and his bride?

Craftman. That when he finds 'twas they were in the carriage, he will curse himself for saving them.

Paul. That's a terrible thing to say, but we certainly are speaking of a terrible man.

Craft. And one whose power will be felt in some frightful way if things go on as they are.

Paul. You're in sympathy with him?

Craft. What do you mean?

Paul. Do you think, with Max, that the line drawn between high and low, in social standing, is a curse, and like him feel that intense hatred of the well-born?

Craft. Am not *I* as good as *Max?* Is not *he* as good as Herr *Brenner?* Aye, even better, for you can surely see that in our sphere there is more heart, more soul, more feeling. Do you deny it?

Paul. 'Tis a lengthy subject, Craftman, and one which some of us had best not think of — but see, the party is already here. [*Exeunt to join crowd.*

Enter CRISTA, RUDOLPH, *the* BARON, *and* OLD BRENNER; *also the Miners. All but* RUDOLPH *display excitement.*

Old B. I regret, my dear Baron, that your first visit to my estate, otherwise so happy, should be marred by what came near being a sad accident.

Baron. No more of the accident, Herr Brenner, please; your son is safe, therefore you should be thankful.

Old B. Yes, Baron, and I am indeed thankful for his escape, as well as for our dear Crista's.

Baron. [*Aside.*] My daughter is not yet so completely a member of his family, that he should speak of her so familiarly. [*Crista looking off at Max.*

Old B. If you will excuse me, Baron, I will precede you into the house. [*Goes in.*

Crista. Did you observe, father, the wonderful physique of that man who stopped the carriage? I tremble still to think of the danger he passed through to save our lives.

Baron. You can scarcely tremble more, my child, than I do at the thought of what you have just escaped. But when I consider the life you are about to take upon yourself, I can but shudder for you and your future.

Crista. Take courage, father.

Baron. That's what I should say to you, my daughter — not you to me.

Crista. I shall be content.

Baron. Heaven grant that you may, for the sacrifice you have made merits far more than contentment. May God give you happiness, my child, if it be possible.

Rudolph. [*Advancing.*] Will you go in, Crista? [*She takes his arm.*] Baron. [*Motioning to Baron who precedes them. They go in.*

[*The miners cheer Rudolph and Crista as they pass in. Rudolph turns, and listlessly acknowledges the demonstration.*]

Craft. Your cheers should be for Max, Max! — he is the real hero of the hour. Where is he?
[*Cries of* "*Max,*" "*Max*"!

Enter MAX. *His head is cut. He has* CRISTA'S *handkerchief. Enter* MINA, *following him.*

Max. Cease calling my name so loud. Would you disturb the noble wedding party with your racket?

Paul. A cheer for Max! [*One loud cheer is given.*

Max. Less noise, I say, to all of you! See that you remember the tawdry event you are here to celebrate.

Mina. Be not so severe, Max. It's all of good intent.

Max. They torment me.

Mina. Do not say so.

Max. They do, I say. They are all thoughtless and inconsistent. They come gladly to assist at this show of aristocracy, and the moment I appear before them there is a shout. They do not know themselves and their own interests.

Mina. Why, Max, you well know that there are many among the men who, filled with the too dangerous advice you have given them, would have gone so far as to turn their backs upon this important event.

Max. [*Sneeringly.*] Important event!

Mina. To the house of Brenner — yes.

Max. Well, let me tell you, child, the time is at hand when the paltry affairs that lie so near the heart of our present chief will be of little consequence to those who share the views of Max Reimer.

Mina. Alas! I know too well and fear what you mean — but, see, the bridal party is returning to the lawn, and you have my lady's handkerchief. Give it me, and I will return it.

Max. I will not.

Enter CRISTA, RUDOLPH, BARON, *and* BRENNER.

Mina. What! — it is my la —

Max. I say, I *will not.*

Mina. What — why — Ma —

[*Retreats as Crista advances.*

Crista. [*Advancing.*] I trust you can and do appreciate it, when I say I am truly grateful — more than grateful for the invaluable service you have rendered Herr Rudolph and me.

Max. I hope that I do, my lady. [*Bows slightly.*

Crista. Can nothing be done to make your wound more comfortable?

Max. Give yourself no uneasiness, my lady. I have only received a scratch, and your words more than repay me for the service.

Crista. Your action was heroic. You will find that my father and — my — husband are as thankful to you as I.

Max. [*Aside.*] Curse her husband.

Rudolph. [*Listlessly and coldly.*] My father's servants are ready to attend you, Reimer, if the hurt you received is troublesome.

Max. [*A little gruffly.*] I do not need them, Herr Rudolph.

Rudolph. I assure you, you have done us great service. I shall gladly make a substantial return for it.

Max. I do not understand you, sir.

Rudolph. You do not understand? You have saved our lives. Is not that *worth* something? I will quickly and with pleasure pay you handsomely.

Max. [*Angrily.*] *Pay me!*

Rudolph. Why certainly, Reimer. Do I put it too plainly to you?

Max. No more plainly than I shall give you an answer, sir.

Rudolph. I must now beg *you* to explain.

Max. What shall I explain, Herr Brenner? I shall never accept any "*substantial return*" from you.

Rudolph. You *will not accept?*

Max. No, sir; no power can make me!

Rudolph. Do you mean to insult me?

Max. If so you must interpret my refusal. [*Turns to exit, sourly. Looks steadily at Crista, as exits. Beckons the workmen. Exeunt.*

Old B. Rudolph, you select the wrong time for such an interview.

Rudolph. Your workman, sir, has insulted me — and in thus beckoning your employés away, he has insulted you also. I presume you will take prompt action in the matter. [*Goes up.*

Old B. My poor, ignorant son. He little knows how impossible it is for me to do anything in the affair; for to implicate myself with this Reimer would —

Enter FRANZ. *He stands by porch.*

Baron. [*Advancing.*] I regret, Herr Brenner, that the time for my departure has arrived.

Old B. Indeed, Baron! and must you go so very soon? Can you not remain?

Baron. I should be glad to stay for Crista's sake; but, thank you, it is quite impossible.

Old B. I very much regret it, my dear Baron. I will prepare at once to accompany you to the station. [*Goes up, sends Franz for coats, etc.*

Crista. [*Advancing.*] I can hardly bear to have you go, father.

Baron. My dear child!

Old B. [*At back.*] And have him drive up at once,
Franz.

Crista. Do beg Harold to come?

Baron. He will, I'm sure. And now, I must say,
farewell, and " take courage " — would that I might be
the all-in-all to you, my daughter, which you so nobly
make yourself to me.

Crista. You are — father — you are.

Baron. Good-bye, my Crista. [*Kisses her tenderly.*

Crista. Good-bye — good-bye — father —

Baron. [*Quietly to her.*] God bless you, my child.
[*She sinks into a seat, and gazes after the Baron.
The Baron bids Rudolph a formal adieu.*

Old B. Do not go in Rudolph — I will join you both
here on my return. [*Exeunt Old B. and Baron.*

FRANZ *enters from having seen the gentlemen to the carriage. He pauses.* RUDOLPH *motions him into the
house.*

Rudolph. [*Seating himself with a bored air beside
Crista.*] Do you not find this eternal parade and cere-
mony very trying, Crista? To me it is intolerable.
Since yesterday noon, we have not been allowed a
moment's peace. First the marriage, then the dinner,
then that tiresome journey, the tragic interlude, followed
by this tedious demonstration just over. Papa, in
sketching the programme for us, seems entirely to have
forgotten that we possessed any such things as nerves;
mine I confess are all unstrung. [*Sighs.*

Crista. [*Distant and reserved, but polite.*] You
might, at least, have offered your reward to the man in
some more delicate manner.

Rudolph. What would you have me do — tender it
to him beseechingly on a salver? I regret that I should
have had the misfortune to offend you in the matter.
Let me have the consolation of your forgiveness
[*Takes her hand, and languidly attempts to put his
arm around her, when she suddenly recoils indignantly.*]
Crista! What — do I again offend you? Is this dis-
agreeable?

Crista. *Unusual,* at least. You have hitherto spared me all this.

Rudolph. *" Hitherto "* — yes, etiquette was somewhat strictly enforced in your father's house. During our two months' engagement, I never once had the happiness of seeing you alone : the constant presence of your father or brothers placed a constraint upon us, which at the present undisturbed interview may well be removed.

Crista. Let me declare to you now that we are alone, that I have no liking for expressions of fondness given, because custom demands them, and in which the heart has no share. I, for all time, release you from this obligation.

Rudolph. You seem in a strange mood to day. " Custom — heart ! " Really, Crista, I believed that with you, least of all, one need have fear of romantic illusions.

Crista. I renounced all my youthful illusions the moment I promised you my hand. You and your father — you would, at any cost, connect your name with the noble one of Rothbart, and thereby force an entrance into circles hitherto strictly closed to you. And, now, you have won your goal. My name is Crista *Brenner!*

Rudolph. You do not appear to like this name ? I had not supposed that compulsion, on the part of your family, led you to take it ; but now it appears —

Crista. *No one compelled me.* No one used over-persuasion. What I have done has been of my own free will, and with a full consciousness of what I was taking upon myself. It was bitter enough for my family to have me make this sacrifice for them.

Rudolph. I do not understand why you take a simple family arrangement so seriously. If my father in this matter had ulterior plans in view, the Baron's motives were certainly of a no more romantic nature — only he might, presumably, have more pressing reasons for the conclusion of an engagement, in which he certainly was not the losing party.

Crista. [*Starting up.*] And you *dare* say this to me, after what happened before your wooing ? I believe that you must blush at this, if you really are capable of blushing.

Rudolph. I must beg you to speak more plainly — I cannot understand your enigmatical words.

Crista. [*Excitedly.*] You know, as well as I, that my family stood upon the brink of ruin! As to whom we owed our misfortune, I cannot and must not judge. It is easy to fling stones at the man who is struggling with destiny. If one inherits his family estates encumbered, if he must uphold the lustre of an ancient name, maintain his position in the world, and secure the future of his children, he cannot heap up wealth like the *Brenners*, in their plebeian gains. You have squandered money from full hands; you have had every wish fulfilled, every caprice gratified. I have tasted the whole misery of a life which feigns and must feign outward splendor to the world, while every day, every hour, brings it nearer to inevitable ruin. Perhaps we might still have escaped, if we had not fallen into *your father's* net. He, from the first, *pressed* his assistance upon us — urged it so persistently that at last he had all in his hands, and we — hunted, entangled, despairing — knew no way of escape. Then he came, and demanded my hand for his son, as the only price of rescue. My father would rather have borne the utmost, than consent; but I would not see him sacrificed — forced from his career. I would not destroy the future of my brothers, and see our name dishonored; and — I gave my consent. What it cost me, no one of my family will ever know; but if I sold myself, I can answer for it to Heaven and my own conscience. You, who submitted to be a tool in carrying out the ignoble plan of your father — you have no right to reproach me : my motives were, at least, more honorable than yours.

Rudolph. [*Slowly.*] I regret that you did not make these explanations before our marriage.

Crista. Wherefore?

Rudolph. Because you would then have been saved the humiliation of being called Crista Brenner. [*Pauses.*] I had indeed no suspicion of these manipulations of my father, as I am accustomed to keep myself entirely aloof from his business affairs. He informed me one day, that if I would go to Baron Rothbart, and sue for his daughter's hand, my proposal would be accepted. I consented to the arrangement, and went through with the formality of an introduction, followed shortly by a betrothal. That is my share in the matter.

Crista. [*Coldly.*] I would have preferred an open confession of your joint knowledge of the transaction to this fable.

Rudolph. So I stand so high in the estimation of my wife, that she cannot even believe my word. [*Bitterly.*

Crista. You must forgive me, if I place no great confidence in you. From that day when you first entered our house — for a purpose of which I am only too well aware — I have only known you from the speech of the city, which —

Rudolph. Painted my picture in no flattering way! I can imagine that. Will you have the goodness to tell me what the city was pleased to say about me?

Crista. They said that Rudolph Brenner indulged in a princely extravagance, squandered thousands upon thousands to purchase the society and friendship of the young nobility, and thereby make the world forget his plebeian birth. They said that in the wild, unbridled life of a certain circle, his life was wildest and most unbridled of all. What else they said about him does not lie within the range of a woman's criticism.

Rudolph. And you naturally do not deem it worth your while to attempt the reformation of a reprobate, over whom public opinion has already broken its staff?

Crista. No.   [*He looks at her face.*

Rudolph You are more than open-hearted! Yet it is always a good thing to know how people stand in relation to each other — and as *we* now stand, so we must remain. The step we have taken cannot be recalled — at least not immediately — without exposing us both to ridicule. If you provoked this scene to show me that I, in spite of the plebeian presumption which won your hand by force, must keep myself, as far as possible, aloof from the Baroness Rothbart — and I fear this alone was your intention — you have won your

goal; but, I beg you, to let this be the first and last of
that sort of

Enter OLD B. *He pauses at back.*

thing between us. I detest all kinds of scenes; my
nerves cannot endure them, and life may be regulated,
so as to avoid these unnecessary *echauffements.* For
the present, I believe I best carry out your wishes by
leaving you. You will excuse me if I withdraw. [*Goes
up ; sees Old B ; stops ; they look at each other.
Crista buries her face.*

Tableau.

CURTAIN.

ACT II.

TWO WEEKS LATER.

SCENE. — *At the mouth of the main shaft of the Brenner mines. Entrance,* C. U., *where machinery for
going down is visible. Above the entrance to the
shaft, a hill rises abruptly toward* L. U. R. *of hill is
long landscape. The scene is of sombre colors, and
the effect is quite dark, although the lights are a
trifle higher than in Act I. The ground is rough,
with large rocks, etc., etc.*

MINA *discovered, seated* R. C. *She has in her hand
a wreath of leaves, which she has been making. She
is singing quietly, as the curtain rises slowly.*

Mina. [*Stopping in her song.*] Heaven only knows
how it will all end! Poor, poor Max! — and yet he is
not to be pitied so much, save for the reason that he
seems to be at war with himself. Would that my heart
were wrong in telling me of the foolish and terrible
passion which I am sure lurks within him. It may
have been sent to prevent him from madly urging on

his followers against the house of Brenner. Max! Max! if my life could pay for making you more of a true Christian, how gladly would I give it up. [*Thoughtfully.*] Can it really be, that he loves —

Enter MAX, L. U.

Max.   Mina.

Mina.   Max! You have not stopped work?

Max.   Preparations are being made for the owner to inspect the elevator. He will come shortly with the director and engineer. I am glad you were here, Mina.

Mina.   You are glad! And why, Max?

Max.   I have something of importance to say to you. Will you listen now?

Mina.   I am always at your service, Max.

Max.   I want to ask you — well I cannot make many words, and between us it is unnecessary. We are the children of brother and sister; we have for years lived together in the same house. You best know what you have to expect from me; and you know that I have always liked you, in spite of the quarrels we have had. Mina, will you be my wife? [*Mina is embarrassed.*

She turns away, and shakes her head slowly.

Mina.   [*In suppressed tone.*] No.   [*Sobs.*

Max.   You will not?

Mina.   No, Max, I will not.   [*Sobbing.*

Max.   Well, then, I might have avoided this long speech. My father assured me that Mina loved me, and indeed I thought you did. Do not be offended at me. I might have realized that I am too wild, too rough, for you. You are afraid of me. You think that after marriage it might be worse. Well — well. In Carl you will find a better man, who will do in all things as you wish.

Mina.   [*Shakes her head — turns toward him.*] I do not fear you, even if you are rough and violent. I know it is your nature. I *would* have taken you, just as you were — indeed gladly — but I will not accept you as you are — as you have been since the day her ladyship came. [*Max is embarrassed.*] Uncle thinks that you care for no one — that you have other thoughts in

your head. Ah, yes! *Quite* other thoughts. You have never cared for me, and now you come all at once and ask me to be your wife. You need some one who will drive away those thoughts; do you not, Max? And for this, the first one at hand will do; for this, I am good enough. But I am not deceived. If I loved you more than all the world, if it cost me my life to let you go — rather Carl, rather any other *now*, than you!
[*Passionately; sobs. A pause.*

Max. Never mind, Mina, never mind. I thought things would be better if you helped me; perhaps, though, they would have been worse, and you are quite right to venture nothing for my sake. Let all remain as it was with us. [*Mina is distressed at this. Exit Mina,* R. U., *sobbing. He breathes a heavy sigh.*] How well she knows you, Max Reimer!
[*Goes up,* R.; *looks off.*

Enter OLD REIMER, L.

Old R. Well, Max, are you ready for the inspection — Heaven grant that it may bring us good fortune.

Max. The men will be here shortly. Father, I have seen Mina.

Old R. You have talked with her?

Max. Yes.

Old R. [*Eagerly.*] Well — [*Seeing Max's face.*] W-e-l-l?

Max. It was of no use. She would not have me.

Old R. Would not have you? Not you?

Max. No. And now do not torment us with questions and speeches about it. She very well knows why she has refused me, and so do I: a third person need know nothing about it. [*Old R. surprised, and starts to speak.*] And now let me go, father — I must go.
[*Exit,* L.

Old R. It's precious little I understood about the matter after all. I thought the girl loved him, but now she refuses him with scarcely a thought. And he — I really did not think the lad would lay it so to heart. He looked quite confounded, and was off like a madman. For my life I cannot account for it, much as I know of him. [*Sighs.*] Well, it's all over, I suppose. Yes — all over. [*Goes up*, L.

Enter OLD BRENNER *and* RUDOLPH, L. *They do not see* REIMER, *who observes them, and exits*, L. U.

Old B. To come directly to the point, Rudolph — what is the trouble between you and your wife?

Rudolph. What is the trouble between us?

Old B. Yes. I thought I should surprise a young married pair during their honeymoon, on returning from town, but instead I find a state of things here of which I certainly did not dream. You ride alone; you drive out alone; neither of you enters the other's apartments. In fact you avoid each other, and when you meet you do not exchange half a dozen words. What does all this mean?

Rudolph. You show a wonderful knowledge of details, sir. Have you been interrogating our servants?

Old B. Rudolph!

Rudolph. An aristocratic mode of life is not understood here, and we are particularly aristocratic in these matters. You love aristocracy so much, father.

Old B. Have done with raillery! Is it with your free consent that your wife ignores you in a way that is even now the talk of the whole colony?

Rudolph. I allow her all the freedom that I enjoy.

Old B. This is too much. Rudolph, you are —

Rudolph. [*Interrupting.*] Not like you, papa; with the promissory notes of her father in my hand, I certainly would have forced no girl's consent.

Old B. What — what do you mean?

Rudolph. Baron Rothbart was ruined. The world knew it. Who was the cause?

Old B. Do *I* know? [*Sneeringly.*] His extravagances — his desire to play the great hereditary gentleman when he was head over ears in debt. He would have been lost without my help.

Rudolph. Really? And did you follow no plan in offering this help? Was not the Baron compelled either to give up his daughter, or be driven to extremities? Did he decide upon this union of his own free will?

Old B. Naturally! Who has told you that it was otherwise?

Rudolph. [*Only slightly more animated than heretofore.*] You knew that I not only did not know or care for Crista Rothbart, but also that I was, before your persistent urging, opposed to marriage at all. It did not please you to tell me what had passed before or after my betrothal. The fact that from Crista's lips I first heard of the business arrangement you had made, ought to explain sufficiently why I decline to expose myself to new humiliations. I have no desire to stand a second time before my wife, as upon that evening when she flung the full weight of her scorn against me and my father, and I — had to remain silent.

Old B. Your silence was —

Rudolph. No, father, words cannot mend matters. The thing is entirely beyond reparation. Therefore let it rest.

Old B. Well, we will talk of this at another time. [*Looks at watch.*] It wants but a few minutes of the time of my appointment to look at the elevator.

Rudolph. "Look at the elevator." And will you not heed what I have said, sufficiently to go into the main shaft?

Old B. No. I will inspect the alterations which have been made in the elevator. What could I do in the mines?

Rudolph. You can convince yourself, if things are really as bad down there as they say.

Old B. What do *you* know about the mines? Who has put this into your head? Has the director thought best to reach my pocket through you? Do not concern yourself. Whatever is absolutely necessary shall be done. I have no money for expensive repairs. I really do not understand why you should trouble yourself about my business affairs. You had best leave to me the care and responsibility in matters of which you do not know the slightest thing.

Rudolph. You are right. "*Not the slightest*" — for that you certainly have cared. Nevertheless, an examination must be made, if for no other reason than to

2

satisfy your rebellious men that the matter of repairs is not wholly overlooked. If you will only go down with the engineer, you can give the shafts a passing inspection.

Old B. I shall be careful not to do that. Do you think I want to risk my life? There is no doubt that things are dangerous in their present condition.

Rudolph. And still you send hundreds of workmen down every day. [*Old B. frowns.*

Old B. Would you give me a moral lecture, Rudolph? You seem to be over philanthropic. Have done with it. In our circumstances it is a very expensive passion.

Enter quickly, WEBER, OLD R., *officers and men.* PAUL, CARL, *etc., etc.*

Weber. Herr Brenner, are you ready?
Old B. Is everything arranged?
Weber. Everything.
Old B. Then I will go down.
Weber. I have here a plan and estimate for further strengthening the machinery of the elevator; will you look at it before descending? [*Old B. does not wish to.*
Rudolph. [*Aside to Old B.*] Do not refuse him.
Old B. Yes; show it to me here. [*Indicating off* R. U. *Weber, Rudolph, Old B. and Officers go off. Workmen busy in preparations.*

Enter MAX, L. U., *who is joined by* CARL, *as he comes down.*

Carl. And do you really intend to keep on, even without the force from the other mines, Max?
Max. "Keep on"—by all means. I tell you *now* is the time—*now* within a day.
Carl. I do not think you have convinced our men of that.
Max. They are cowards—all of them. They cannot stir from their places, by reason of their irresolution and timidity. They know, as well as I, that we ought to avail ourselves of this very hour; yet they will not go forward, because they are alone—because the others will not stand by them. It is a lucky thing that we

have Brenner against us, and no other. If he were a politic man, who at the right time showed us his teeth, and at the right time gave us encouragement, we could bring nothing to pass.

Carl. Do you think he will do nothing, then?

Max. No: he is cowardly, like all tyrants. He swaggers and threatens while he has the upper hand; but if his skin or his gold sacks were in danger, he would crawl on his hands and knees. He has made himself so thoroughly detested, he has so goaded the miners to extremities, that at *last* not one will remain behind. Then, we shall have him in our hands.

Carl. And the young gentleman? Do you think he will take no part when the riot breaks loose?

Max. [*With contempt.*] He counts for nothing. At the very first alarm he will run back to the city for safety. If we had to do with him it would be soon over.

Carl. Will Herr Brenner go into the mines, do you think?

Max. [*Laughs.*] What are you thinking of? Do you suppose he would risk his life? No, indeed. I wish I could have him alone there once, eye to eye; he should teach me that trembling we so often endure below. [*They go off* L. U. *followed by others.*]

Enter CRISTA *and* BARON, *with* FRANZ.

Franz. This is the place, your ladyship.

Crista. Very well, Franz. Find Herr Brenner, and say that the Baron awaits him here. [*Exit Franz,* R. U.] Was not Count Reynau's death very sudden, papa?

Baron. Very, my child. He was in perfect health not ten days ago, and his contemplated marriage was to have taken place within a month.

Crista. His marriage? How strange it seems. Is it not astounding that this should have occurred, and at such a time? We never could have hoped for the heirship.

Baron. Never! Reynau was young and healthy; he was about to marry. And now! Oh, Crista, it is *distracting* to think of inheriting this large estate after it is too late, and I have sacrificed my child.

Crista. O, papa, you need not think of me. I — I
breathe freely to think you will have so abundant a
recompense for the humiliations you have suffered.

Baron. If his death was decreed, why, why could
it not have happened sooner? One month ago it would
have saved us. One quarter of the wealth now flowing
in upon me would have been enough. That our sacrifice
should have been made in vain! This mockery of fate
I cannot bear!   [*Takes her hand — embraces her.*

Crista. You should not speak so, papa. This death,
which, knowing what Count Reynau was, we can mourn
only formally, frees you from many burdens. My marriage averted only the most threatening: there still
remained enough that pressed heavily upon us, which
later might have brought you into humiliating depend-
ence upon that man. This danger is now forever averted.
You can repay all you have received from him. We
owe him nothing more.

Baron. But he owes you to us, and he will guard
against ever paying the debt. That is why this rescue
galls me. A short time ago I should have greeted it with
transport : now it drives me to despair on your account.

Crista. I am, perhaps, not so unhappy as you and
my brothers believe.

Baron. Aren't you! Do you think your letters
have deceived me? I knew beforehand that you would
spare us the knowledge of your trials; but if a doubt
had remained in my mind, your paleness speaks plainly
enough. I know how much you must have suffered,
and do still suffer.

Crista. I fear you may exaggerate. I have no com-
plaint to make of Rudolph. He has from the first
maintained a distance, for which I can but thank him.

Baron. I would not advise him or his father to forget the respect they owe you — to fail in appreciating
the honor you have brought to their house, where hitherto little has been found. But, Crista, I can at least
offer you one consolation : you will not long bear the
name to which attaches so much vulgarity — so much
villainy against us and others. I have taken care that
this plebeian title shall not much longer annoy you.

Crista. [*Surprised.*] Why, father, what do you mean ?

Baron. I have entered upon the necessary steps for — your — your — husband's elevation to nobility. Only his elevation, not his father's : Brenner, I would not recognize even formally, as belonging to our rank.

Crista. If you wish the title of nobility on my account, papa, you err. Still you are right, and in any event it is best. The title will amply compensate Rudolph for all he must renounce. [*Baron surprised.*

Enter, R. U., BRENNER, RUDOLPH *and officers.*

Old B. My dear Baron, I beg you will pardon our unavoidable delay. Believe me, I am glad to see you with us again. [*Offers hand to Baron, who accepts coolly.*

Rudolph. [*Advancing.*] Your unexpected visit is certainly a pleasure, Baron. [*Sees that officers are watching, so offers hand — formal greeting.*

Old B. [*To Crista.*] I am sorry you had the trouble of coming out. We should have returned soon.

Crista. Thank you, Herr Brenner ; but the Baron has only a short time to remain, and he wished to see your son. [*Retreats a little.*

Enter at back, L. U., MAX, CARL, PAUL, CRAFTMAN *and miners.* CRISTA *recognizes* MAX.

Old B. I beg you to excuse me for a few moments, Baron, as I must make an examination of the elevator. I will see you at the house soon.

Baron. Certainly.

Old B. [*To Weber.*] Let me go down now, quickly. [*Rudolph listless ; he watches Crista, as she looks at Max. Old Brenner and officers approach the shaft.*

Weber. Reimer, are you ready to accompany our chief ?

Max. I attend him, sir.
[*As he comes forward, he passes near Crista.*

Crista. Are not you the man who rendered us great service on the day of our arrival ?
[*Preparations making at shaft.*

Max. It was I who had the privilege to stop your horses, my lady.

Crista. Whatever has been said or done regarding the matter, I thank you now again, most heartily.

Max. You are very kind. I am *more than* repaid [*glances in direction of Rudolph*] for what was but a trifle.

Crista. Do you not fear so constantly descending into the mines?

Max. What use would it be to fear it, your ladyship? *We must live.* If my death is to come from such a cause, I am perhaps fortunate that it is to be so sudden and soon over. [*Salutes her respectfully; looks her in the face; goes up.*

Crista. Papa, do you not see something almost grand about that man?

Baron. He has a remarkable physique, and more dignity than I have ever noticed in a workman.

Crista. I cannot but admire him, and yet he seems like a dangerous man. [*More aside to Baron.*] Is he not a striking contrast to [*indicating Rudolph*] his superior?

Baron. He is, indeed! [*Brenner and Max sink into the shaft. Men grouped. Officers talking together. Rudolph advances.*

Rudolph. [*To Baron.*] Before we go to the house, Baron, may I ask why your visit must be brief?

Baron. I left the city to attend the funeral of a relative, Count Reynau, whose residence is about ten miles from here. I must return at once.

Rudolph. I trust you will accept my sympathy, sir. He was not nearly related?

Baron. He was a cousin, and circumstances connected with his life make it impossible to regret his death. Herr Brenner, I bring tidings from the city, which for you must be of the highest interest.

· *Rudolph.* Indeed, sir!

Baron. I may well assume that the wish of your father, in regard to an elevation of rank, has been no secret to you, and I can assure you that its fulfilment is at hand. In one point of view there are certainly insuperable obstacles — there are certain prejudices against the elder Herr Brenner, personally, which can scarce be surmounted; but the powers that exist are quite ready to distinguish one of our first industrial proprietors, by conferring a title upon his son. I hope, in a short time, to be able to congratulate you. [*Rudolph has listened with but little interest. As the Baron stops, R. looks up and at him. Crista intently watches Rudolph.*

Rudolph. May I ask, Baron, if in this matter you have been governed solely by the wishes of my father, or by consideration for your daughter?

Baron. [*Embarrassed.*] When this union had been once decided upon, your father's wish and mine became the same, but I did not at that time conceal from Herr Brenner my opinion concerning his personal claims to that dignity, and I received from him the assurance that, if necessity required it, he would renounce the honor in favor of his son.

Rudolph. Then I regret that my father did not inform me of the progress of an affair which I regarded only as an undeveloped plan; and I regret still more, Herr Baron, that you have used your influence to secure for me an honor which I must absolutely decline.

Baron. [*Amazed.*] Pardon me, Herr Brenner! I might not have heard distinctly. Did you speak of *declining?*

Rudolph. I did. I decline the title most absolutely.

Baron. I entreat you, then, to give me the reasons for this, to say the least, *strange* refusal. I have great curiosity to know.

Rudolph. The strangeness lies less in my declining than in the manner of the offering. If a title of nobility had been decreed to my father, on account of the service he has undeniably rendered to industry, as his heir I should in any event have accepted it. They have not thought best to confer it on him, and I have not the slightest claim to such an honor; I therefore deem it better not to let society assert that an alliance with the Rothbart family must, as a natural consequence, be followed by a diploma of nobility.

Baron. Your views seem to have undergone a change since your marriage.

Rudolph. [*Smiles sardonically.*] Before my marriage, Herr Baron, I had not learned how I was regarded by your circle. Recently, and in rather a merciless way, all this has been made clear to me; and you cannot be surprised if I decline henceforth and forever to be considered an intruder into that circle.

[*Crista displays emotion, and turns her back.*

Baron. I have no idea who has thus been exaggerating matters to you, but I must beg you to have some regard for Crista. In the role, which you expect to play next winter in the city, she cannot — pardon me, Herr Brenner — wear your plebeian name. That was not intended by your father or me.

Rudolph. Our winter circumstances may not be what we now expect. Leave that to Crista and me. For the present nothing remains to be said, but that I persist in my refusal of a distinction which — pardon me — I will not owe to the aristocratic name of my wife!

Baron. Your conduct, Herr Brenner, is — [*Noise of accident in the shaft. The elevator has fallen. Max has escaped injury. Old Brenner has been killed instantly. The officers disappear in assisting. Miners rush to entrance of shaft. Max's voice is heard — "Help." General alarm.*

Weber. [*Appearing quickly.*] Herr Brenner! Herr Brenner! Your father! [*Disappears.*

Rudolph. What is it? What has happened? [*Disappears after Weber. Baron goes up; he beckons Crista to remain at distance.*

Baron. [*Coming down.*] Crista, I cannot help feeling that there is an end to hatred and hostility between the elder Brenner and us.

Crista. Do you think it is serious, father?

Baron. I think this accident has caused his death!

Officers and men appear with RUDOLPH, *bearing body of* BRENNER.

Rudolph. Has a physician been summoned?

Weber. Alas! Herr Rudolph, it is too late.
Rudolph. Father! father! He is dead!

> [*Kneeling over him.*

> *Enter* MAX, *from shaft.*

> [*Crista moves toward Rudolph, and stands by him, with head bent down. She makes an effort to appear the "devoted wife." Max stands aloof, excited and defiant. Officers near Rudolph. Miners grouped, and watching all intently.*

CURTAIN.

ACT III.

SCENE. — *A handsome library in the Brenner mansion. It is elegantly, but not gaudily, furnished. Large door,* L.; *smaller door,* R.; *large bay window,* C. *back. Desk up,* R. C. *Sofa, chairs, etc., etc. Fireplace,* R.

KLASSEN, WEBER, KELLNER *and four officers discovered.*

Klassen. You are indeed right, Schäffer. Since the death of Herr Brenner there has, even in the two weeks past, been a noticeable feeling of relief, in spite of the garbs of mourning which are not yet thrown off.

Schäffer. To me it is a problem to understand and solve. Herr Rudolph may be weak and inexperienced, but it surely cannot be expected that he will close his ears to the counsel we are in a position to give him, and which will practically place him in the position his father maintained.

Weber. Ah, Herr Schäffer, there you touch upon the vital point, for Max Reimer is the very man to take all possible advantage of the weakness of our chief; and where the head is weak, subordinates are powerless.

Klassen. And then, Herr Schäffer, we should not be so hasty in condemning our new chief. We hardly know him yet. What did he say when you informed him of the state of affairs?

Schäffer. Nothing. He took the papers I gave him, and, thanking me, shut himself up with them. Since then I have not seen him.

Klassen. Well, we shall soon see him in his real colors. The demands Reimer has presented require the utmost care and judgment; and our engineer has spoken truly of this man, for you see he puts forth his arguments at the very moment when we are weakest.

Weber. He is a thorn in our flesh. Without him the workmen would be reasonable. We cannot blame them for demanding security for their lives, and wages that will keep them from starvation; but they should have stopped with the demands it is possible to grant. What they dictate under this man amounts to an open insurrection.

Kellner. But what will the young chief do? Will he accede to their demands?

Weber. That he most certainly *cannot* do. It would subvert all discipline, and in less than a year make him a ruined man.

Schäffer. Yet he has scarce any other alternative. We have, of late, had serious losses, and the actual existence of the works depends upon an uninterrupted continuance of business. Let them lie idle but a short time, we cannot fulfil our contracts — and that would be ruin.

Weber. The trying position in which the young chief finds himself would, I fear, be more than he could bear, if he had a suspicion of the connection Reimer is said to have had with his father's death.

Schäffer. Do you really believe in the possibility of a crime?

Weber. The inquest has only established the fact that the rope was broken. To be sure, it *might* have become broken of itself; as to this, Reimer alone can say. In any other companionship there would have been no suspicion, but *he* is capable of anything.

Schäffer. But then, think that he too was in danger of losing his life. The spring with which he rescued himself was a desperate venture, and could not have been accomplished by one man in ten.

Weber. You little know Max Reimer, if you believe he would for one moment hesitate to risk his life in undertaking anything which imperilled it. Think of how he flung himself before the horses. At that time the whim seized him to save life; but if he wishes to destroy, it matters little to him whether his own destruction is threatened. That is just the dangerous thing about this man: he has no regard either for himself or others; in a case of necessity he would sacrifice himself, if —

Enter RUDOLPH. *He looks pale. In his hand are papers and documents. He wears mourning. Formal salutation. He goes up to desk.*

Rudolph. I have summoned you, gentlemen, to take counsel with you in business matters, which since my father's death have fallen into my hands. There is much to adjust and change — more, perhaps, than we at first supposed. I have, as you know, hitherto stood remote from business circles, and shall not at once see my way clearly [*the officers show some surprise, and begin to grow more interested*], although in these last days I have sought to do so. I depend, therefore, in the fullest measure upon your good will and your readiness to sustain me. I shall be obliged to lay much claim to both, and beforehand, I assure you of my thanks. [*Officers acknowledge.*] All other matters must of course recede before the momentary calamity — the danger with which the demands of the miners, and cessation of their work in case of refusal, threaten us. There can be thought or mention here of but one decision. [*Schäffer glances at Weber.*] Before all things we must inform ourselves how the men are organized, and who leads them. [*A pause.*

Weber. They are led by young Reimer, Herr Brenner, and there is no doubt that the organization is well led and perfect in all respects.

Rudolph. That I also fear; and it is positively evident that there must be a fight, for there can naturally be no talk of granting these demands in full. [*Sits.*

Weber. Naturally there can be no talk whatever of it, Herr Chief.   [*He looks at Schäffer.*

Rudolph. Before going further has our director any general opinion to express?

Klassen. Thank you, Herr Brenner. I cannot but think we should gain much by a diplomatic course of inaction for the present.

Rudolph. And you, Herr Schäffer?

Schäffer. Owing to the present condition of the works, and the absolute necessity for continuing our contracts, it is impossible for me to see how we can do aught but submit. In faith, I feel quite certain that *we must.*

Rudolph. [*Specially dignified.*] I must request you to use more considerate language, Herr Schäffer. Indeed we *must not* submit. There are other than moneyed considerations — the first of all being that of my position among the miners, which would be forever insecure if I now yielded to their mercy. Little as I understand such things, I see that these demands far outstretch the bounds of possibility. And you must all agree with me in this. There may be wrongs and inconveniences. The workmen are doubtless justified in asking for examinations and repairs in the mines, and an increase of wages. They may also well speak of certain alleviations, and of fewer working hours; but all beyond this is arrogant defiance.

Weber. For which their leader, Reimer, is alone responsible.

Rudolph. As he is the leading spirit in the revolt, we had best first listen to him. I have already sent him word to meet us here, and to bring some of his comrades with him, adding that they should be received as ambassadors. Will you summon them, Herr Kellner?

[*Exit Kellner. Officers gather* R. *Weber on* R. *of Rudolph.*

Re-enter KELLNER, *followed by* MAX, CARL *and* CRAFTMAN. KELLNER *retreats to* L. *of* RUDOLPH. MAX *stands* L. C., *and* CARL *and* CRAFTMAN L. U., *near* MAX.

Rudolph. [*Stands.*] Steiger Reimer, you laid before

me yesterday, through our director, the demands of the miners upon my works; and in case they are not granted, you threaten a general cessation from work.

Max. That is so, Herr Brenner.

Rudolph. Above all things, I desire to know if you really intend that I shall regard your proceedings as a declaration of war, for they amount to nothing less. Even you must say to yourself that I cannot grant such things, and will not.

Max. Whether you *can* grant them I do not know, Herr Brenner, but I believe you *will* grant them, for we are determined to let the works lie idle until you yield to our demands: substitutes you cannot find in the whole province.

Rudolph. [*Firmly.*] It is by no means my intention to refuse all your demands. There are among them some whose justice I recognize, and to which I will also yield. The examination and repairs of the mines shall be granted; the wages will, at least, partially be raised. To do this I shall be obliged to make heavy sacrifices, more perhaps than from a business point of view are justifiable at present; but it shall be done. But you must relinquish the other points, whose sole aim is to take the management out of the hands of my officers, to relax the discipline, which in an enterprise like this is a question of life or death.

Max. [*Somewhat amazed. He stares at officers and at Rudolph.*] I am sorry to tell you that these points will not be abandoned.

Rudolph. I really believe that these minor points are the main thing with you, but I repeat, they *must* be abandoned. [*Gazes steadily at him.*] In my concessions I will go to the utmost limits of possibility; but there I shall stand and take no step beyond. What I concede shall and must content every one who seeks honorable remunerative work. I give my word that everything necessary for the safety of the workmen, and for the raising of their wages, shall be done; and now I demand from you some confidence in my word. But before we go further you must renounce the second part of your demands. Their fulfilment is impossible, and I enter into no agreement on that score.

Max. [*Enraged.*] But you shall not refuse in this way Herr Brenner! There are a thousand of us, and the works are just as good as in our hands. The time has passed when we allow ourselves to be enslaved and trod upon just as it pleases you. [*Rudolph advances.*] We now demand our rights; and if we cannot win them by fair means, we will take them by force! [*Makes a rush for Rudolph, as if to grab him by the throat. The officers rush toward Rudolph — Weber first. Rudolph waves back officers with right hand, and gazes steadfastly into Max's face. Max shrinks back with a muttered vow. Carl and Craftman amazed at Max. Pause. Tableau.*

Rudolph. [*Coolly.*] Before all things, Reimer, change the tone in which you address your chief! If you would be received here as an ambassador, and as such would claim a sort of equality, then behave yourself, and do not hurl your threats of force and insurrection into one's face. You demand obedience from your men; I demand it from you. Play the master among your comrades if it so pleases you, but remember that while I stand before you *I* am master of these works, and intend to remain so! Rely upon that! — and now inform your comrades what I will and what I will not grant them, and add that I will not take back a single word I have said. With this we are for the present at an end.

[*Turns — goes up.*

Max. We are; and I declare to you in the name of all the associated miners upon your works, that from to-morrow every man will be idle.

Rudolph. It is well. For that I am prepared. See to it that order is maintained. You cannot intimidate me by tumultuous scenes. If you force it upon us, we shall have a long and bitter conflict. Think well before you act.

Max. We shall see who holds out the longest! Come! [*Exit, followed by Carl and Craftman, who show timidity.*

Rudolph. There are two already who follow him with

only half a heart. I hope the majority will come to their senses when we have given them time; for now, gentlemen, we must yield to necessity, and let the works lie idle. I in no way ignore the danger which threatens us here — in the withdrawal of a thousand men, with a leader like Reimer at their head — but I am resolved to maintain my stand. It naturally depends upon your own free will whether you follow me. As you were nearly all against my decision, I of course shall not force its results upon you, and willingly give leave of absence to any of you who may deem a temporary withdrawal necessary.

Schäffer. There is not one of us who would accept, Herr Chief!

Rudolph. Then I deeply thank you, gentlemen. I must leave you now. Herr Schäffer, in an hour I will meet you in my cabinet. Herr Kellner will please remain here a moment. [*Exit* R. *door. Officers, except Kellner, exit* L., *talking.*

Kellner. Heaven, Heaven, what a scene! I tremble in all my limbs! I thought that wild man, that Reimer, would rush upon him any minute. But that glance! — that way of speaking — why he's a regular Henry Fifth, right from the pages of Shakespeare — from history itself.

Enter FRANZ.

Franz. Excuse me, Herr Kellner, I supposed Herr Brenner was here.

Kellner. He is in the next room, Franz; do you wish to see him?

Franz. Yes, sir; I thought he would like to know that her ladyship has been gone some time on a ride alone.

Kellner. What! alone?

Re-enter RUDOLPH.

Rudolph. What are you saying, Franz?

Franz. That her ladyship has been out nearly an hour, sir, unattended.

Rudolph. Alone?

Franz. She declined an escort, sir.

Rudolph. Indeed! There is danger in such a ride, now. Have my horse brought immediately to the side porch. I will take the main road. You and Anton may go by the cross road as quickly as possible.

Franz. Reimer's niece, Mina, is here, and asks to be allowed to see you, sir.

Rudolph. Send her to this room; Herr Kellner will see her for me. [*Exit Franz, L.*] Will you not?

Kellner. Certainly, Herr Chief—by all means.

Rudolph. Thank you. [*Exit quickly, R.*

Kellner. Her Ladyship riding alone! Strange! But for Mina, I too would seek her.

Enter MINA, L.

Mina. Ah, Herr Kellner, I thought Herr Brenner—

Kellner. Yes, he was obliged to leave, and asked me to see you.

Mina. This handkerchief, you may remember, was given to Max by her ladyship at the time of the runaway. I have secured it, and came to give it back; if not to her ladyship, then to the chief.

Kellner. I will take care of it for you.

[*She gives it to him.*

Mina. I was in hopes, too, that I could learn directly from Herr Brenner something of what Max has said and done. Can you tell me? Uncle is sorely troubled.

Kellner. Alas, Max is very aggressive. He and Herr Brenner had a stormy scene here just now.

Mina. Indeed! so I feared. Are they not likely to be reconciled?

Kellner. Not unless Max finds his senses.

Mina. Alas, alas! It seems as though he never would. But give her ladyship the handkerchief. I did not think it best—that is, I was resolved that Max should keep it no longer.

Kellner. Did he desire to keep it?

Mina. Yes.

Kellner. Yet he hates the Brenners.

Mina. He hates the husband, but the wife—

Kellner. [*Lackadaisically.*] Her ladyship is an angel, while Max is —

Mina. Not deserving of utter condemnation, Herr Kellner. He is a man of soul, and for much of his terrible nature he is not at all responsible.

Kellner. Your pardon, Mina; and what do *you* think of her ladyship?

Mina. She is very beautiful.

Kellner. Is that all you think of her?

Mina. Why do you ask me? You must certainly know that one cannot speak highly — if from the heart — of such a wife as Lady Crista is.

Kellner. I know it, Mina, I know it.

Mina. Kindly deliver the handkerchief for me. I must return.

Kellner. I am going, and will accompany you.

[*Exeunt.*

Enter CRISTA *and* RUDOLPH, R.

Rudolph. How very imprudent it was in you to ride out alone to-day. You certainly had no suspicion of the danger. I started immediately upon hearing of your caprice. Franz and Anton have also gone in the direction of the works.

Crista. But I should have shunned the highway if you had not joined me. I was already warned.

Rudolph. Warned? By whom?

Crista. By Reimer himself, whom I met in the forest.

Rudolph. [*Starts.*] Reimer? And did he dare approach and speak to you, after all that has happened of late?

Crista. It was only to warn me, and to offer me his company and protection. I declined both; that I believed I owed to you and to your position.

Rudolph. [*Sarcastically.*] You believed you owed it to me? I am infinitely obliged to you for this deference; it is well you showed it; for if you had let him escort you, much as I wish to avoid giving the first occasion for conflict, I should have made him sensible that the inciter, the ringleader of this whole rebellion, had best keep his distance from my wife. [*Pause; goes to window.*] I am sorry I was obliged to shorten your ride: it is certainly a charming day.

Crista. [*Seated* R. C.] I fear a ride in the open air was more necessary to you than to me. You look so pale, Rudolph.

Rudolph. I am not accustomed to work. [*Ironically.*] It all comes from effeminacy. I cannot, even for a short time, perform the labor my officers do daily.

Crista. On the contrary, it seems to me that you are working beyond what is required of any one. All day long you scarcely leave your work, and at night I see your light burning until morning.

Rudolph. For how long a time have you so attentively scrutinized the windows of my apartment? [*Bitterly.*] I did not believe they really had any existence for you.

Crista. Since I knew that the danger, which you persistently denied, every day grew nearer. Why did you conceal from me the magnitude of this conflict, and its possible results?

Rudolph. Because I did not wish to alarm you.

Crista. I am not a timid child, whom one must surround with such anxious care. If any danger threatens us —

Rudolph. [*Coming down.*] *Us?* I beg your pardon; the danger threatens me alone. I have never thought to treat you as a child; but I considered it my duty not to enlighten the Baroness Rothbart in regard to matters which must be indifferent to her, and which in a short time will be as foreign to her as the name she now bears. [*Coldly.*

Crista. Do you deny me all information in regard to your affairs?

Rudolph. Not if you desire any.

Crista. [*Pause.*] Have you refused your miners their demands?

Rudolph. What I could grant, and what the workmen of themselves asked, I have granted. With Reimer's extreme demands I can do nothing. Their necessary consequences, if granted, would be the subversion of all discipline. They would end in anarchy; and they are really insulting. He would not have dared make them had he not known what I have at stake in this contest.

Crista. What have you at stake — your fortune?

Rudolph. And my life!

Crista. Yet you will not yield?

Rudolph. [*Very firmly.*] No!

Crista. I fear that Reimer will pursue the quarrel to extremities: he hates you.

Rudolph. [*Disdainfully.*] I know it. The sentiment is mutual.

Crista. You should not underrate this man's hatred, Rudolph. He is terrible in his passion, as in his energy.

Rudolph. Do you know him so well? But a short time ago you thought this blouse hero worthy of your admiration — a low, worthless energy — that which scorns impossibilities, and would rather drag hundreds into ruin than listen to a word of reason; but even Reimer may find a wall against which his stubborn obstinacy will beat in vain. He will force nothing from me. I will fight the battle through, even to my own overthrow.

Crista. When we just now met Reimer and his men in the road I thought they certainly would not let us pass. Their menace showed me the very great danger of your position.

Rudolph. I must bear it. You have seen what blind obedience this man knows how to enforce. A word from him and they let us ride on unhindered; not a single one dared murmur, and yet they were only waiting a signal from him to assail us.

Crista. [*Musingly.*] But he did not give the signal.

Rudolph. No, not *to-day.* He best knows what restrained him. But he will to-morrow, or a day thereafter, if we chance to meet again. I am quite certain of that. [*Approaches her chair.*

Crista. Do you really believe he would? [*Her hand rests on the arm of the chair; as Rudolph draws near her, he puts his hand on hers.*

Rudolph. Does it frighten you, Crista? **Are** you alarmed?

Crista. [*With feeling.*] Rudolph, I —

Enter FRANZ, L., *quickly.*

Franz. Herr Baron Rothbart and his son have arrived. [*Rudolph quickly leaves Crista's side; he looks annoyed. Crista disappointed at interruption.*

Enter HAROLD, L., *in uniform.*

Harold. My dear sister! [*Embraces her.*
Crista. Ah, Harold, is it you? [*Exit Franz, L.*
Harold. [*Shakes hands with Rudolph formally.*]
Pardon me if I have intruded Herr Brenner, but I have not seen Crista for so long.
Rudolph. Certainly. You are quite welcome.
[*Goes toward* R.
Crista. Will you not remain?
Rudolph. Pardon me if I beg you to receive your father alone. I had forgotten something which I must attend to. I will, as soon as possible, pay my respects to the Baron. [*Exit Rudolph,* R. *Harold looks angrily at him as he exits. Crista intently watches him off.*
Harold. [*Turning to Crista.*] Crista, I am delighted to see you again?
Crista. [*Forces a smile. Her eyes are on the door through which Rudolph left.*] I, too, am delighted to see you. Inexpressibly delighted? Why does not father come up?
Harold. Here he is.

Enter BARON, L.

Baron. My dear Crista!
Crista. Father! [*They embrace.*
Baron. How is my noble daughter? [*They sit.*
Crista. I am well, father — very well.
Harold. You do not seem so, Crista? [*Sits.*
Crista. I am perfectly well, Harold.
Baron. When your surroundings are different, I shall hope to see more color in your cheeks, Crista.
Harold. Something of permanent benefit must be done for you.
Crista. Enough of me. Tell me, father, how you happened to come so soon. Have you been to the Reynau estates?

Baron. We are now returning from there, and could not resist coming by way of this place, for your sake and our own. But tell me, will you not listen to the subject which is uppermost in our minds?

Crista. I know well what you mean. You speak of a — separation ? [*Looks down.*

Baron. Yes, my child; a separation, no matter under what pretext, or at what price. Those who are forced to a thing are wont to hold to it only through compulsion : now that I am master of my affairs, now that I need no longer be under obligation, I will venture all to release you from those fetters which you assumed only for my sake, and which, whether you admit it or not, make you infinitely unhappy.

Harold. It is not a new thought to you, is it, Crista? Father has talked of nothing else for some time. It must be that you desire it.

Baron. What did Old Brenner not resort to in order to obtain this union with us ? The possibility is not imaginable that he would have allowed a divorce which would have excluded him from that circle to which he had forced an entrance through us. His sudden death has charged all; but the opposition of the son remains to be overcome.

Crista. He will yield. You need have no anxiety on that account.

Harold. So much the better. So much the sooner it will be over.

Baron. It must be your wish, Crista, as well as ours, that this painful transaction be conducted and terminated as speedily as possible. I think you had better return with us to the city, and from there take the necessary steps. You can then simply decline returning to your husband, and await the decree of divorce. We will take care that he does not violently assert his rights. [*Rises.*

Harold. Yes, by Heaven, we will! If he should refuse to undo this shameful business, your brother's sword will compel him to it. He cannot threaten us with disgrace and public humiliation, as his father did.

Crista. Recall your threats, Harold, and you, father, banish your anxieties. Both are unnecessary. This divorce, which you think must be a matter of strife and compulsion, has long been a settled thing between Rudolph and me. [*Baron and Harold start up in amazement and listen intently.*] We had agreed upon this even before Herr Brenner's death; but we wished to shun the publicity of so sudden a rupture, and therefore decided to preserve the outward restraints of a married life.   [*Her voice trembles.*

Harold. Even before Brenner's death!   [*Rises.*

Baron. And you yourself had spoken of the matter? You were decided upon it?

Crista. [*Struggles to gain full possession of herself; rises.*] I have never introduced the subject. It was Rudolph who, of his own free will, offered me the separation.

Baron. What! It was *he himself?* Is it possible?

Harold. Well, it is all the same, sister dear, so long as he gives you back to us. In the enjoyment of the new inheritance, you have everywhere in it all been wanting to us. [*Embraces Crista; she buries her face on his shoulder.*

Baron. What is the matter, Crista?

Crista. Forgive me, papa, if I seem strange to-day. I am not quite well. At least, not well enough for a conversation on this subject. You must permit me to withdraw. I —

Baron. You have suffered too much of late, I can easily see. Go, and leave all to me. I will spare you as much as possible.

[*Exit Crista, handed to door by Baron.*

Harold. This is very singular, father. Do you comprehend this Brenner? I am sure I do not.

Baron. [*Pacing to and fro.*] I will speak with him, and if he really is of our mind, which, notwithstanding Crista's assertion, I must still doubt, the business shall be entered upon immediately.

Harold. Immediately? Why they have not been two months married, and I think they are right in trying to avoid too early and abrupt a separation.

Baron. Certainly they are, my son, and I should agree with you, were it not that I have been told the trouble now threatening on Brenner's premises is very dangerous for his business and his fortune, and you can easily see that in the event of a collapse, his wife could not leave him then — in the face of the world she could not. It is better for us to assume the responsibility of too early a rupture than to have our hands tied when the dreaded catastrophe really comes. Crista must return to our house, must be free before there is a suspicion in the city of how matters stand here.

Harold. It is strange that Crista enters into the matter with so little heart. She is cold and silent, as if this lay remote from her — as if it dealt with almost anything but her own freedom.

Baron. She suffers at the thought of the unavoidable publicity, and the anticipation of annoyances which cannot be spared her. It is a painful step for her, but it must be taken. We shall certainly have the sympathy of all our friends. The reason of the marriage could have been no secret, and all will readily comprehend why we seek to dissolve it.

Harold. When Brenner comes, father, shall I not leave you alone with him?

Baron. No, Harold, you will remain. You are the —

Enter RUDOLPH, R.

I trust you are well, Herr Brenner.

[*Salutes at distance.*

Rudolph. Thank you, quite so. I am glad you could favor us with a visit — and you especially, Herr Harold; are you not fatigued after your journey? [*Formally.*

Harold. Not at all, thank you. We experienced a very comfortable jaunt.

Rudolph. I trust you will excuse me for not joining you sooner. Business matters have required a great deal of my attention at all hours. I presume Crista's presence has fully compensated you. Indeed, I thought she was still with you.

Baron. Crista has withdrawn on account of a slight indisposition, and with your permission I will employ the opportunity of her absence to express a wish, the fulfilment of which depends principally upon yourself.

Rudolph. [*Motions the Baron to seat. Harold goes to window at back, and stands facing off* R.] You have only to state your wish, Baron, if the granting of it depends upon me.

Baron. There must be greater significance placed upon the rebellion at your works, I think, than it really deserves. Yesterday, as I stopped at the town to call on the commander of the garrison there, who is an old friend, I was told that the outbreak of your workmen into open insurrection, requiring military interference, was very probable.

Rudolph. People in the town seem to be more occupied with my works and my workmen than I had supposed. At all events, I have not called on the colonel for assistance.

Baron. For myself, I naturally have no opinion in the matter; I would only seek to remind you that it will not be proper to expose Crista to possible outbreaks. I very much desire to take my daughter home with me for a time, until matters have become settled.

Rudolph. [*Suppresses his emotion.*] Crista is entire mistress of her own actions. If she thinks the removal necessary, I give her perfect freedom.

Baron. Then she will accompany us to-morrow. As to the duration of her visit there, we come to a point painful for us both to discuss; but I prefer to treat with you by word of mouth, especially, as I know that in the main our wishes coincide.

Rudolph. Very well, Baron. I presume that Crista has already communicated with you.

Baron. She has.

Rudolph. I supposed that the matter would remain a secret between us until the time for action came. I see I have erred.

Baron. Why defer the carrying out of a conclusion once fixed upon? This is a favorable time. The present condition of your estates gives us the best and plainest excuse for my daughter's removal. The world need not, at first, know that this removal is to be a permanent one. [*Pause.*

Rudolph. [*Pause.*] Does the wish for this haste come from Crista herself?

Baron. I speak in my daughter's name.

Rudolph. [*Starts up — goes to fireplace.*] I consent to all, Baron — to all. I thought I had stated to your daughter my reasons for delay. They were, for the most part, dictated by regard for her. If, regardless of these, she still wishes matters accelerated — let it be so.
[*Harold turns and looks front.*

Baron. You also unconditionally agree to the separation?

Rudolph. I do.

Baron. I am very grateful to you, Herr Brenner. [*Rises.*] Ahem! There is one thing which still remains. Your — father — had the goodness to assume certain obligations for me, which at that time I could not fulfil. I am now in a position to do this, and I would like to —

Rudolph. [*Looks at him.*] Had we not better let this matter rest? For my part, I implore it.

Baron. It might rest so long as our mutual relations remained as now — not when they were dissolved. You will not oblige me to remain your debtor.

Rudolph. This cannot be called a debt in the usual sense. My father, at the last, only enforced his own demands, and the documents were destroyed as soon as [*excitedly*] the price for them was paid!

Baron. At that time the agreement was closed at Herr Brenner's expressed wish — now it is to be dissolved mostly at our wish. Circumstances are changed.

Rudolph. Is it absolutely necessary that in this divorce business we hold fast to the conditions of a bill of sale? I hope that for the second time my wife and I shall not be made the objects of a business transaction.

Baron. Be pleased to remember, Herr Brenner, that the term "business" has relation to only one of the two parties; it does not apply to us.

Rudolph. I am now fully aware, Baron, how this marriage was brought about, and I know how those obligations arose which forced you to consent. This being the case, you can well appreciate my demand that the

debt shall not be alluded to — not even by another syl-
lable. I demand from you, Herr Baron, that you do
not force a son to blush at the remembrance of his
father !

Baron. I did not know that you looked upon the
subject in this light. [*Turns to go.*] Before I retire,
allow me to say that I had no intention of wounding
you, but —

Rudolph. That I assume. [*Rings for servant.*] And
now grant me the favor of forgetfulness in regard to it
all. As to this divorce, I will instruct my lawyer to
meet every step of yours. If anything is required of
me personally, I beg you to command me.

Enter FRANZ. RUDOLPH *beckons him to attend the*
BARON *and* HAROLD.

I will do everything in my power toward gaining the
desired end speedily and considerately.

Baron. I thank you.

Harold. I also thank you, Herr Brenner—good night.

Rudolph. Good night. [*Exit Baron, Harold and
Franz. Rudolph walks to window ; pushes shut-
ters together; walks back to fireplace; rings for
servant.*

Re-enter FRANZ.

Rudolph. Close the room, Franz — leave the light
on my desk. [*Rudolph leaning over fireplace. Franz
secures windows, and puts out gas.*

Franz. Anthing further, Herr Brenner ?

Rudolph. Give orders to have a carriage in readiness
for the morning train. Her ladyship is to leave for a
visit to the city with her father, brother and maid. That
will do — I do not wish to be disturbed again. [*Franz
bows and exits. Rudolph walks to and fro ; stops
at mantle and takes down picture of Crista ; looks
at it ; heaves a sigh and replaces it; walks to
window and gazes out.*

Enter FRANZ, *cautiously.*

Rudolph. [*Turns quickly.*] What is it ? Have I
not given orders ?

Franz. I — I — beg your pardon, Herr Brenner, I know that you do not wish to be disturbed; but — as — her ladyship herself —

Rudolph. Who?

Franz. My lady herself is here, and wishes —

Enter CRISTA. *Exit* FRANZ.

Rudolph. [*Hands her in.*] Do you have yourself announced? What superfluous etiquette!

Crista. I heard that you would see no one, and Franz told me the order was for all, without exception.

Rudolph. I am sorry that you could not voluntarily consider yourself an exception.

Crista. I wished to speak with you.

Rudolph. I am quite at your command. Will you not be seated? [*Hands her to seat.*

Crista. Thank you. I will not detain you long. [*She hesitates and seems embarrassed.*] My father has just told me of his conversation with you, and of its result.

Rudolph. I expected this; and it was on this very account that — I beg your pardon, Crista — that I was at first surprised to see you here. I believed you busy in preparations for departure.

Crista. You have already announced my departure to the servants?

Rudolph. Yes: I supposed I anticipated your wishes. In any event, I thought it better to have the announcement made by me. You of course know the pretext we employ. If you designed conducting the affair in any other manner, I regret not having known your intention.

Crista. I have nothing to suggest to you. It only surprised me that the time of my departure, once firmly agreed upon, should be hastened. You certainly had the same reasons for holding fast to that decision as at first.

Rudolph. I? It was your wish, your demand, to which I consented. At least, Baron Rothbart told me this was so.

Crista. I suspected this. My father has gone too

far, Rudolph. He has spoken in my name when he
only expressed his own wishes. I have come to explain
this misunderstanding, and to tell you that I will not
go — at least not until I hear from your lips that you
demand it.

Rudolph. You will not go? And why not?

Crista. You yourself told me that in the struggle
before you your life was at stake. Since your last meeting with Reimer I have known that the battle must
be fought to the bitter end, and that your position is far
more dangerous than you will admit to me. I cannot
and will not leave you at such a moment: it would be
cowardice and —

Rudolph. You are very magnanimous; but in order
to practise magnanimity, you must find some one who
will accept it, for I will not accept yours.

Crista. [*Excitedly.*] You will not?

Rudolph. No. The plan emanated from your father :
let it stand! He has doubtless a right to provide for
the protection and security of his daughter, who will
belong to him, from the barbarities and excesses which
may soon happen here. I give him full power, and
agree to to-morrow's separation.

Crista. And I consent, only so long as I consider it
your wish. I will not yield, in this matter, to the dic-
tation of my father. I have taken upon myself the
obligations of your wife, at least before the world; and
before the world I will carry them out. They command
me not to desert you in the hour of danger, but to remain
at your side until the catastrophe is past, and the time
of our separation originally agreed upon has arrived.
Then I will go, but not before.

Rudolph. Not even if I imperatively demand it of
you ?

Crista. Rudolph!

Rudolph. I have told you to play no magnanimous
rôle with me. They cannot move me. *Duties!* A
wife, who of her own free will gives a man her hand and
heart may well deem it her duty to remain by her husband in danger, to share his misfortune, perhaps his
ruin. This certainly is not your case. We have no

duties to each other, because we have had no right in each other. The only solace I could offer you in this enforced marriage was the possibility of its dissolution: it has been dissolved since that moment when we agreed to a divorce. That is my answer to your proposition.

Crista. You should not make remaining so difficult for me. You must know, Rudolph, the struggle it cost me to come to you in this way. Will you not consider it?

Rudolph. I do not doubt that the Baroness Rothbart makes an incalculable sacrifice in deciding for a few months longer to bear my plebeian name, and to remain by the side of a man she so thoroughly despises, even though he offers her immediate freedom. I was once compelled to hear how terrible both were to her, and can therefore estimate what this self-sacrifice costs.

Crista. You taunt me with the conversation upon the evening of our arrival here. I — I had forgotten that.

Rudolph. Had you really? You do not ask whether I have forgotten it. I was obliged at that time to listen to your words; but they went to the utmost limit of what I could bear. Do you imagine that a man would with impunity allow a woman to tread him in the dust as I was trodden that evening, and then permit her to lift him up again, if it happened to please her to change her mind? I am not quite the miserable weakling you thought me. From that hour I ceased to be so. That hour decided my character; but it also decided our future. I have learned a great deal of late: I shall carry through this contest — but [*standing*] the woman who, on our marriage day, with such annihilating scorn, thrust me from her, not even asking if the husband to whom she had just given her hand was really as guilty as she believed him; who took my assertion, made upon my word of honor, that I had known nothing of my father's share in that marriage transaction as the subterfuge of a *liar;* who in reply to my question whether she did not deem it worth her while to attempt the reformation of such a reprobate as I, flung forth a disdainful "*No*" — this woman I will not have at my side when I fight the battle for my future — I will be alone!

[*Takes stage ; goes to window at back ; pause.*

Crista. [*Suppressed emotion.*] You will stand alone! Well — then — I will not obtrude myself upon you. I came to convince myself whether my father's plan was yours also. I see that it so — and I will leave you. [*Goes toward* L. *door. As she does so Rudolph is drawn toward her, bringing him near chair,* R. *She pauses at door, and turns slowly.*] We shall meet to-morrow only in my father's presence ; and then, perhaps, never again. So — farewell!

Rudolph. Farewell! [*Exit Crista,* L.] *My God!*

[*Sinks into chair.*

CURTAIN.

ACT IV.

SCENE. — *The interior of the engineer's headquarters at the mouth of the mines. Office furniture, mining instruments, etc., etc.; door* R. C. *in flat, large window* L. C., *table* L. C., *high desk* L.; *stools, chairs, etc.; maps and plans hung on walls. Signal bells* L. *of window. Screen,* R. *of door.*

RUDOLPH *and* WEBER *discovered.*

Weber. I am certainly the last man, Herr Brenner, who would advise outside assistance, but I think you have done enough to restrain the revolt. You cannot be blamed for resorting to a measure which, in previous cases, has been taken much earlier and with no such urgent necessity as ours.

Rudolph. Previous cases can be no rule for us. A few imprisonments and a few shots would count for nothing here, where Reimer stands at the head. He would not quail before a bayonet charge, and with him also stand or fall his entire band. If we should resort to military force, peace for us could only come over the bodies of the slain. If I allow even a shot to be fired, then I am the tyrant who allows murder in cold blood — the oppressor who takes delight in destruction. The old overseer once said to me — and they were no idle words — "If rebellion once breaks out among us, then God help us!"

Weber. But if peace is not to be obtained otherwise?

Rudolph. Peace cannot be secured by force. For the moment I might subdue the insurrection, only to have it the next year, perhaps the next month, break forth anew; and you know as well as I that this will take from me the last possibility of holding the works. The distrust so many years sown among the miners cannot easily be uprooted, especially as no reconciliation with Reimer is to be hoped for. This I know, as I have sought it myself in vain.

Weber. You have sought it yourself?

Rudolph. Yes, in an accidental meeting with Reimer yesterday, I once again offered him my hand.

Weber. Is it possible? And yet, in truth, you know nothing!

Enter CRISTA. *She goes behind screen.*

Rudolph. [*Surprised.*] Why, what do you mean? You may be assured, sir, that I know how to fully maintain my dignity even on such an occasion as that.

Weber. I beg your pardon, Herr Brenner — my expression was not intended as a criticism on our chief: it referred only to the son, who certainly has no suspicion of the reports connected with his father's death.

Rudolph. Why — you speak of my father's death and refer to Reimer; is there any connection between the two?

Weber. I fear so. Indeed, we all fear it. Common suspicion attaches to Reimer, and not alone with us — his comrades also entertain the idea.

Rudolph. [*Excitedly.*] At that time in the mines? A treacherous attack on a defenceless man? I cannot believe that of Reimer!

Weber. He hated your father, and he never denied

his hatred. Whether the rope really broke through mere accident, and he employed the moment of danger to rescue himself, and hurl his chief back into the abyss, or whether the whole was a deliberate plan — this question truly is shrouded in mystery: but he is not innocent; for that I would vouch.

Rudolph. The inquest decided that it was an accident.

Weber. The inquest decided nothing. They assumed it to be an accident, and let it pass as such. No one ventured a public accusation. Every proof was wanting; and pursuing the matter would hardly have done any good. We knew, Herr Brenner, that as things then were you could not avoid a conflict with this rival, and we would at least spare you the bitterness of knowing with whom you fought. That was the cause of our silence.

Rudolph. I did not suspect that — not that! And even if it is only a suspicion, you are right: I should not offer the man my hand.

Weber. And this man has, at the head of his comrades, brought all this misfortune upon you and us. He has incessantly fermented and prolonged the quarrel; and now, when his power is declining, he seeks to make the rupture incurable and reconciliation impossible. Would you spare him now, if you could?

Rudolph. Spare him? No! And I can no longer spare the others either; they drive me to extremities. This very morning two hundred men wished to resume work; and they certainly have a right to demand protection for their work. The mines must be made secure at any price: I cannot accomplish this alone, and —

Weber. We await your commands, Herr Brenner.

Rudolph. I will write at once to General Berger. It must be so!   [*Sits to write.*

Weber. [*Aside.*] *At last!* It is, indeed, high time.

Rudolph. Go, please, and take care that all the officers remain at the posts which I assigned them. They must not move until I come myself. This morning it would have been useless to interfere in the tumult. Perhaps it is now possible. In half an hour I will be with you. Meantime, if Reimer and his band make any move whatever, send me word at once.

Weber. I know what this decision costs you, Herr Brenner, and you may feel assured that none of us take the matter lightly; but we need not always fear the worst, perhaps it will all pass over without bloodshed.

[*Exit quickly, not observing Crista.*

Rudolph. [*Pauses in writing; folds letter, and puts it in his pocket; rises; takes stage; stops — thoughtfully.*] And so! a new trial — murder? — murder? — can it — be —

CRISTA *comes out.*

Crista. Rudolph!

Rudolph. Crista! Crista! you here? Pray how was it possible — for what —

Crista. I came only a few moments ago. I certainly had to win my way by force; do not now ask me how; it is enough that I won it. Rudolph, I wanted to come to you before danger reached you.

Rudolph. What does this mean, Crista? I wish for no sacrifices from duty and magnanimity. I told you that when you went away, three days ago.

Crista. Yes, I know it. With these words you have once already thrust me from you. You could not forgive me for having once done you wrong, and in revenge for that you had almost sacrificed yourself and me. Rudolph, who was the more revengeful — the harder — of us two?

Rudolph. It was not revenge — I gave you freedom: you had yourself wished it.

Crista. If I now tell my husband that I will not have this freedom without him, that I have come back to share all with him, whatever may happen, that I — have learned to love him — will he then for the second time bid me go?

Rudolph. [*Embraces her quietly — fervently.*] My wife!

Crista. Rudolph!

Rudolph. You come like an angel from Heaven, Crista. [*Takes her to seat.*] Tell me, why did you come in here instead of going to the house.

Crista. I had much trouble getting through the grounds, and was obliged to accept the assistance of our

4

fiercest enemy. I paused here in the hope of finding an escort for the rest of the walk. Matters seem to be in a startling condition — tell me all, Rudolph.

Rudolph. Reimer and his followers are likely at any moment to break forth. I am obliged to visit the works continually in person. Indeed, I must go now for a few moments;—yet I cannot leave you here alone.

Crista. No, Rudolph, I shall not keep you from your duty, though my heart trembles at your exposing yourself. You will hasten back?

Rudolph. Indeed I will, darling, and take you to your home — our home. [*Kisses her.*] Good-bye.

Crista. Good-bye. [*Exit Rudolph. Goes to table ; sits thoughtfully — happily.*] Crista Brenner! Crista Brenner! Now do you regret breaking away from what *was* your home, to come to what *is* your home! How I shudder to think of the almost narrow escape! What a blessing it was that father did not suspect my departure. He would have forced me to sign that terrible plea for a separation, which would have been my death knell. Dear father! He shall soon learn his mistake, or else lose his daughter forever. [*Goes to window.*] How careless it was in me to let Rudolph go out, perhaps to come face to face with the mob. I cannot remain here. I must seek him. [*Starts to go.*] No, no, foolish girl that I am. It *cannot* be that he will come to harm.

[*Looks out window.*]

Enter MAX *quickly.* CRISTA *startled.*

Crista. Who's there? Reimer!

Max. Your pardon, my lady. I little expected to find you here — I seek Herr Brenner.

Crista. I did not suppose that after all that has happened you would seek to enter any apartment of your chief. You must know that he can no longer receive you.

Max. It is for that very reason I seek to speak a few words with him. I expected to find him alone. It was not you I sought, your ladyship.

[*Advances toward her.*

Crista. [*Retreats.*] Ah!

Max. [*Laughs.*] Can an hour have made such a change? But now you demanded my protection, and leaned upon my arm as I conducted you through the tumult: and now you flee from me, as though your life was in danger.

Crista. Leave me! My husband is not here! You see that he is not; and even if he were to come now, I should not leave you alone with him.

Max. Why not? *Why not?*

Crista. Because your nearness has already proved fatal to a Brenner.

Max. [*Startled.*] Ah, that was it. I might have known that this would find its way to you.

Crista. Reimer, can you pronounce the reports false, which since that unhappy hour have been connected with your name?

Max. And even if I did, would you believe me? [*Pause ; more earnestly.*] Would you believe me?

Crista. I hold you capable of crime when your passionate nature is aroused, but not of falsehood.

Max. As it is you, my lady, who asks, I will answer.

Crista. It is declared to my husband that it was more than a mere accident which caused the rope to break on that unlucky day. Was it so?

Max. It was an accident, or rather it was something better, if you will force me to say it — it was retribution. Our chief had caused a change to be made in the elevator, which, like all he did was for necessity, not for security. What mattered it if a few hundreds of miners, who must every day go up and down this elevator, were every day exposed to danger. Double and treble what it was able to bear was demanded of the machine, and it at last had its revenge, but not upon the workman — it was upon the chief himself. It was not a human hand, my lady, which made the rope break just at that moment when it must bear his weight ; and it was mine least of all. I saw the danger coming: we were already at the last platform ; I made a spring upward, and —

Crista. Pushed him back?

Max. No! I only let him fall. I could have rescued him if I had wished. A half minute was time enough for that. In truth, it might have cost my own life; he might have pulled me down with him if I had come to his help; for every one of my comrades, for any one of the officers, I would have gladly taken the risk; but for that man *I would not.* At that moment all he had done to us shot through my brain. I thought that the fate, to which every day he had exposed us, was only coming to him; and I would not interfere with the just retribution of Heaven. In spite of his outcries I did not lift my hand, and a minute after it was too late. The elevator fell, taking him to his death.

Crista. Have you told me the whole truth, Reimer? Upon your honor?

Max. Upon my honor, your ladyship!

Crista. And why did you not solve this mystery by speaking to others as you have to me?

Max. Because no one would have believed me — not a single one, not even my father.

Crista. You should have forced them to believe you, Reimer, and they would have done so if you had only seriously demanded it; but your pride and obstinacy would not suffer this. You met the suspicion with disdain, and thereby strengthened it. Now you are suspected throughout the works by the officers, by my husband —

Max. What do I care for Herr Brenner? what for all the rest? Whether they condemn me or not, it is all the same to me. But I could not bear, my lady, to have you turn from me in fear and detestation; from you alone I could not bear it; and you believe me now: I see it in your eyes. I am perfectly indifferent to the rest.

Crista. I believe you, and I will see that my husband exculpates you from the worst suspicion at least. We must not judge you for failing to save life where you might have done so; for that you are answerable to your own conscience. But Herr Brenner shall no longer believe that the murderer of his father stands opposed to him. You have certainly gone too far now for reconciliation. For the first time, within this hour, I have learned all that has happened — all that perhaps will happen if the attack upon the mines is renewed. [*Lays her hand thoughtlessly, imploringly on his arm.*]

Reimer, we stand upon the brink of a fearful catastrophe. You have forced my husband to protect himself and his from danger, and he has concluded so to do. Within a few hours, perhaps, blood will flow, must flow; reflect upon whom the responsibility will fall.

Max. Upon me, do you think? Have a care, my lady! It might also fall upon you, if it harmed the one you love. Herr Brenner certainly will not remain in doors if there is fighting outside; that I know, and I also know whom I shall first seek when the conflict breaks out. [*Crista retreats.*

Crista. Reimer, you speak with the wife of your chief! If you hate him —

Max. [*Passionately.*] The chief? It matters not with whom I at the head of my comrades have to deal. It is Rudolph Brenner I hate, because you are his wife, because you love him, and I — I *love* you, Crista, more than all else in the wide world! Do not be so horrified at this; you must have known it long ago; I could not help it from the first moment I saw you. I have tried by force to crush and annihilate this love, but I could not. I cannot to-day, even though I again feel more than ever the old truth that only equal must unite with equal, and for such as I there can remain nothing but an aristocratic shrug of the shoulder, even though we have perilled life itself for her we love. But if a life is again in peril I am not the one so senselessly to expose my own as I did under the hoofs of your horses; for that, another life than mine must be risked. I have already hated a Brenner to the death; I then believed I could hate no man on earth so bitterly: now I know better. I have not yet been guilty of murder; but there is one I could murder — one only! I did not kill the father; but if I should ever be thus alone with the son, then it would be he or I, or both! [*He starts towards her, and tries to get her hand. She struggles away from him, and*

RUDOLPH *enters.*

He rushes up to them, pushes Reimer back violently, and clasps Crista with his left arm, producing pistol in his right hand, which he points at Max.

Rudolph. Back, Reimer! Do not again attempt to approach! One more step toward my wife — a single one—and you lie upon the floor!

Max. I've no weapon. Were I armed, then we should stand equal against equal. You have better prepared yourself than I. I have only my fist to place against your pistol, and there is no doubt which would do the quickest work. [*Crouching.*

Rudolph. It is your doing, Reimer, that we must now always have loaded weapons in our hands. I will at least protect my wife against you, even if it costs your life. [*Reimer starts forward a little.*] Back, I tell you once again!

Max. I have never yet placed much value on my life, but I will not allow myself to be shot down under a roof of yours. I have still to reckon with you. Do not tremble so, my lady. [*Goes toward door.*] You are in his arms, and he is safe; *now* he is safe, but we are not yet at an end. And even if you both stood there linked together for all eternity, still some time my hour would come; and then, then you would think of me!
[*Exit.*

Rudolph. Do not tremble, Crista; it is over.

Crista. Would that it all were over. You came at the right time, Rudolph.

Rudolph. What did he wish here?

Crista. I do not know. He sought you, but evidently with no good intention.

Rudolph. What induced him to attack you in that manner?

Crista. He was in a state of frenzy. Some other time I will explain what he said. On some accounts we should pity him, Rudolph. Oh, I am so thankful you were here to meet his attack.

Rudolph. I fear it was only a prelude to the real drama, which seems to be very close at hand. Do you fear it, Crista?

Crista. I fear nothing more at your side. But, Rudolph, do not again go out alone in the midst of the uproar as you did just now. He is there, and he has sworn your death.

Rudolph. [*Looks into her face.*]. Life and death are not in Reimer's hands, my darling — over them is another who must decide. Be calm, Crista! I will but do my duty; but I shall do it otherwise than in all these days before, for I now know that my wife is anxious about me. That I shall not easily forget.

Enter KELLNER *hastily.*

Kellner. Herr Brenner, I have come — my lady! — I beg pardon. I have something very urgent to tell you, Herr Chief.

Rudolph. Speak out, Kellner. I keep nothing from my wife. Speak quickly. [*Cheers are heard in the distance — very indistinctly.*

Kellner. Those cries, Herr Brenner, are in praise of Max Reimer, who has almost this moment taken his place among the miners, and ordered an approach to this building we are in! I hastened before the officers; they are here.

Enter WEBER, KLASSEN *and other officers.*

Rudolph. [*Coolly.*] Well, Herr Weber?

Weber. Reimer's rage is at its height. He and his men are approaching. [*Cries heard nearer.*] Some immediate action must be taken. The troops are not yet due. [*Cries nearer.*

Rudolph. I will face them alone.

Officers. Alone!

Crista. No, Rudolph, no — you shall not!

Rudolph. [*Aside to her.*] The time has come for courage, Crista. God grant you plenty. Stay my noble girl. I shall be safe. [*Cries heard.*] Your calmness will be an invaluable aid. My wife! [*Caresses her.*] Not one man shall go from this room until I give a signal. [*Goes to door.*] Herr Weber, see that no one stirs from here. [*Exit, going off* L. *by window.*

Kellner. My soul! what a man!

[*Crista and others looking eagerly out of window.*

Klassen. Heaven help him. We must not — I cannot stay here.

Weber. We should be doing wrong to go — it would spoil all! We must stay.

Crista. See! See! He confronts them! They seem subdued almost with his first word. Brave, brave man! Hark! what does he say? Oh, that I could hear him!
Weber. [*Starts.*] Great Heaven! words are no longer of avail, they are turning on him. Come! [*Exit quickly, followed by all except Crista. The officers just get in front of the window when*

THE EXPLOSION

occurs. Two or three glaring flashes of light from L., *accompanied by a terrific sound like hollow thunder, followed by a long rumbling noise. The officers are at first struck dumb and motionless; then they rush off, not observing Crista, who reels and faints at the first shock, but does not shriek. Cries outside of, " To the main shaft!" " To the main shaft!" " Stand back!" Other cries, and then "Reimer!" "Reimer!" A pause; then*

Enter RUDOLPH *quickly; his coat is soiled, and he wears no hat; he sees Crista lying on the floor; is startled; says nothing at first, but rushes up to her, and raises her head to his breast.*

Rudolph. [*Softly — quietly — distressed.*] Crista!
Crista. [*Quietly; opens her eyes, and looks into his face with an expression of relief.*] Safe!
Rudolph. Safe and unharmed.
Crista. [*He helps her to a seat.*] What was that terrible shock, Rudolph?
Rudolph. Terrible indeed, my darling. The changes of years seem to have been wrought into a moment. I had almost given up all hope, and saw the men furiously rushing toward me, when suddenly, and by a Mighty Hand, came that shock. All were as still as death; then it dawned upon a hundred minds at once that an explosion had occurred in the mines.

Enter WEBER, KELLNER, MINA, OLD REIMER *and miners.*

Weber. Thank heaven, the mine was empty.
Rudolph. My God, no, it was not. I had forgotten

the miners who went down to resume work this morning. [*To Weber.*] Can the cage be lowered ?

Weber. No; the chain is broken in the shaft. If some man dared go down and mend the break —

Enter KLASSEN.

Rudolph. I will. [*Goes toward door.*]

Crista. No! no!

Klassen. That is being done.

Weber. By whom ?

Klassen. Max Reimer.

Enter miners, supporting REIMER.

Klassen. The broken chain ?

Reimer. [*Gasps.*] It is mended. [*Slips from the miners' hands and falls. The others gather round.*

Mina. [*Bending over and caressing him.*] Max! Max! He is dying.

Crista. [*Approaches Reimer — stoops over him.*] Reimer, are you much wounded ?

Max. [*With much effort.*] Why do you ask after me ? You have *him* again. Why should I want to live ? I have already said to you, "he or I." I then thought 'twould be different — but — it — cannot — be changed — — I am sat-is-fied! [*Falls back dead. Crista rises, and joins Rudolph. Mina and Old R. bending over Max. Miners and officers grouped. Crista and Rudolph looking down at Max.*

CURTAIN.

THE END.